He's Been a Monster ALL Day!

By Denise Brennan-Nelson Illustrations by Cyd Moore

I wonder why Mommy
thinks that of **me?**
I guess if she does,
then a **monster I'll be!**

I'm big and **Strong** — I grumble and **growl**

and scare people off with a **Sneer** and a **Scowl**.

My **fangs** can chop metal. One **oogly eye.**

Dinosaur **scales** and maybe I **fly?**

I'm no longer **scared** of what's under my **bed**.

He's now my **pet** monster. I'm calling him **Ted.**

Mud baths for me
all **gooey** and **slimy**.

No need for soap—
monsters are **grimy**.

I drive monster trucks all **revved up** and **loud.**
Mom won't be happy, but Dad will be **proud.**

I stay up all night having **fun** in the **park**.

No monster I know is **afraid** of the **dark**.

Discover a cave—
hide-and-seek with the **cats**.

We put on a show
and wear silly **hats**.

Eat bugs and lizards, fat worms and **snails.**

Gobble up spiders and **salamander tails.**

Forget about manners.

No "**thank you**" or "**please**."

I wouldn't mind playing with someone, **but who?**

Seems no one likes monsters.
What should I **do?**

I order my favorite
ice cream piled **high**.
Can't finish it all
as much as **I try**.

Wish Mommy were here.
Wouldn't be all **alone**.
Together we'd finish
this **monster-sized cone**.

Being a monster
isn't so **great**.
I'm going home—
hope it isn't too **late**.

Tomorrow she'll see
a **monster I'm not!**

Maybe by now

Mommy **forgot**.

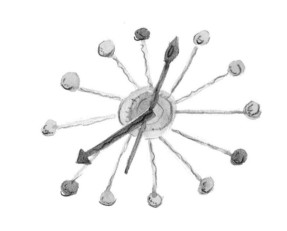

Warm, cozy blanket. Pillow so **soft**. Hear Daddy's voice as I'm **dozing off...**

"Look at him now, **sweet as can be.**

For Hayden, Julian, Cecilia, and Mickenzie.
Love, Aunt Denise

For my friend Denise, whose words stir
the imaginations of all of us monsters!

Cyd

Sleeping Bear Press
315 E. Eisenhower Parkway, Suite 200
Ann Arbor, MI 48108
www.sleepingbearpress.com

Printed and bound in the United States.

10 9 8 7 6 5 4 3 2 1

Library of Congress Cataloging-in-Publication Data

Brennan-Nelson, Denise.
He's been a monster all day! / written by Denise Brennan-Nelson ;
illustrated by Cyd Moore.
p. cm.
Summary: After hearing his mother say that he is a monster, a little boy
decides to prove her right over the course of one loud, grimy, scowling day.
ISBN 978-1-58536-827-3
[1. Stories in rhyme. 2. Behavior—Fiction. 3. Monsters—Fiction.] I. Moore, Cyd, ill.
II. Title. III. Title: He has been a monster all day!
PZ8.3.B7457He 2013
[E]—dc23
2012033686

JUN 2 8 2013